PURNELL
LITTLE READERS

Titles in this series:

The Good Old Rocking Horse
Dame Roundy's Stockings
The Bear with Boot-Button Eyes
The Little Sugar Mouse
The Dog with the Long Tail
The Goblin and the Dragon

Enid Blyton's
The Good Old Rocking Horse
and other stories

Enid Blyton's
The Good Old Rocking Horse
and other stories

PURNELL

SBN 361 03230 7

Published in 1975 by Purnell Books, Berkshire House,
Queen Street, Maidenhead, Berkshire.

Text © 1975 by Darrell Waters, Limited.
Artwork © 1975 by Purnell & Sons Limited.

Made and printed in Great Britain by Purnell & Sons Limited,
Paulton (Somerset) and London.

CONTENTS

Please Shut the Gate   11

The Wishing Carpet   15

The Little Toy Maker   35

Angelina and the Toy Balloon   41

Betsy-May and the Bear   47

The Good Old Rocking Horse   53

The New Doll   60

Please Shut the Gate

"There's a dear little baby kid at the farm," said Mother to Ted and Tessie, just as they were about to set off to school one morning.

"A tiny little goat!" said Tessie. "Oh, I would so like to see it. Ted, let's hurry, then we can ask the farmer's wife if we can go and see the little kid."

"Now have you both got your satchels?" called Mother. "Is your mid-morning lunch in them? Have you got your homework with you, and your pencils and rulers?"

"Yes, we've got everything!" called back the twins and ran off in a hurry. They came to the farm and saw Mrs. Straw feeding her hens.

"Please may we see the baby kid?" asked Tessie.

"Of course," said Mrs. Straw. "It's in the little field, there, with its mother. But please shut the gate, dears—I don't want the nanny-goat let out."

The children ran off to the little field. They put down their satchels on the grass and opened the gate between them, because it was rather stiff. Then they saw the little kid, and cried out in delight.

"Oh, it's like a toy one! It's simply sweet. Oh, if only it belonged to us!"

The kid was tame and friendly. The children spent five minutes playing with it and then said good-bye and ran out of the field to collect their satchels again.

Then they saw a dreadful sight. The nanny-goat had gone out of the gate and was standing over their satchels. She had eaten all their biscuits. She had also eaten Ted's number book and Tessie's writing book. She had even eaten Ted's rubber! And she was just about to chew up his best pencil when he shooed her off.

Tessie ran crying to Mrs. Straw. "That horrid nanny-goat came out and ate our biscuits! She's eaten some of our books."

"Miss Brown will be very cross," said Ted. "Will you smack that goat hard, Mrs. Straw? Now we shall have to buy new pencils and books and we have no biscuits for lunch."

"Now how did she get out of the field to eat all that?" asked Mrs. Straw. "Who could have been silly enough to leave the gate open? For otherwise she could not have got out."

Oh, dear—the two children went very red and didn't say another word. Who left the gate open? Why, they did, of course.

The Wishing Carpet

Once upon a time there were two children who owned a wishing carpet. A little old woman had given it to them in exchange for a basket of mushrooms. They had met her on Breezy Hill when they were gathering mushrooms, and she had begged them to give her their basket.

"Here you are, my dears," she said, when they handed her their mushrooms. "Here is something in exchange for your mushrooms. It is a magic carpet. Take great care of it."

They took it home and unrolled it. It was bright blue and yellow, with a magic word written in green round the border. Peter and Betty looked at the carpet in wonder.

"I say!" said Peter. "Suppose it really is magic, Betty! Shall we sit on it and wish ourselves somewhere else and see what happens?"

"Yes," said Betty. So they sat themselves down on it, and Peter wished.

"Take us to the big city of London," he said. The carpet didn't move. Peter spoke again.

"I said take us to the big city of London," he said, more loudly. Still the carpet didn't move. It was most disappointing. And no matter what the two children did or said it just lay still on the floor and behaved like any ordinary carpet.

"It isn't a wishing carpet, after all!" said Betty, disappointed. "That old woman wasn't telling the truth."

"What a shame!" said Peter. "Let's roll it up and put it in our toy-cupboard. We won't tell the grown-ups about it because they might laugh at us for believing the old woman."

So they rolled it up and put it right at the back of the toy-cupboard. They forgot all about it until about four weeks later when they met a very strange-looking little man in their garden.

"What are you doing here?" demanded Peter.

"Sh!" said the little man. "I'm a gnome. I've come to speak to you about that magic carpet of yours."

"It isn't a magic carpet at all," said Peter. "It's a fraud. It won't take us anywhere."

"Show it to me and I'll tell you how to make it take you wherever you want to go!" said the gnome eagerly.

"Come on, then," said Peter, and he led the way indoors. But on the way Betty pulled at his sleeve.

"I don't like that little gnome at all," she said. "I'm sure he is a bad gnome, Peter. I don't think we'd better show him the carpet. He might want

to steal it."

"Don't be afraid," said Peter. "I shall have tight hold of it all the time!"

He led the way to the toy-cupboard and pulled out the carpet. He laid it on the floor and then sat on it. The gnome clapped his hands in joy when he saw it and sat down too.

"Come on, Betty," said Peter. "Come and sit down as well. This may be an adventure. Oh look, here's Bonzo, the puppy. He wants to come as well! Come on, Bonzo, sit down on the carpet too."

So Betty and Bonzo sat down beside the gnome and Peter.

"Did you say the magic word that is written round the border of the carpet?" asked the gnome.

"Oh, no!" said Peter. "I didn't know I had to."

"Well, no wonder the carpet wouldn't move then!" said the gnome. "Listen!"

He looked closely at the word round the carpet border, and then clapped his hands twice.

"Arra-gitty-borra-ba!" he said. "Take us to Fairyland!"

In a trice the carpet trembled throughout its length, and then rose in the air. It flew out of the window and rose as high as the chimney-pots. The children gasped in astonishment and held on tightly, afraid of falling off. The carpet flew steadily westwards.

"Oh!" said Peter. "So that's how you do it! My goodness, what an adventure! Are we really going to Fairyland?"

"Yes," said the gnome. "Keep a watch out to the west. You will soon see the towers and pinnacles on the borders."

Sure enough it was not long before the children saw shimmering towers and high-flung pinnacles far away on the blue horizon. The carpet flew at a great speed, and the world below seemed to flow away from them like a river, so fast were they going.

"Fairyland!" cried Betty. "Oh, how lovely!"

They soon passed over a high wall, and then the carpet rapidly flew downwards to a big square that seemed to be used for a market. And then something dreadful happened.

The carpet had hardly reached the ground when the gnome gave Peter a hard push that sent him rolling off the carpet. Bonzo rolled off too —but Betty was still on it with the gnome.

"Ha! ha!" cried the gnome. "I'm off with Betty! She shall be my servant! I've got the carpet for my own, foolish boy! Arra-gitty-borra-ba! Take me to my castle, carpet!"

Before Peter or Bonzo could pick themselves up and rush to reach the carpet, it had once more risen in the air and was flying high above the chimney-tops. Peter groaned in despair.

"Oh dear, oh dear, whatever shall I do? Betty felt certain that the gnome was a bad old fellow, and I didn't take any notice of her. Now he will make her his servant and perhaps I'll never see her again!"

Bonzo put his nose into Peter's hand, and, much to the little boy's surprise, he spoke.

"Don't worry, Peter," he said. "I expect we'll get her back again all right."

"Good gracious, you can speak!" cried Peter in surprise.

"Well, we're in Fairyland, you see," said Bonzo. "All animals can speak there."

Peter looked round the market square. He saw many pixies, elves and brownies looking at him, and he went up to some of them.

"Could you please help me?" he asked. "My little sister has been taken away on my magic carpet by a horrid little gnome. I don't know where he's gone to, but I really must get Betty back again. She will be so frightened all by herself."

"How dreadful!" cried the fairy folk. "Why, that must have been Sly-One! He lives in a castle far away from here. Nobody dares to go near him because he is so powerful."

"Well, I must go and find him," said Peter bravely. "I've got to rescue my sister. Tell me how to get to Sly-One's castle."

"The Blue Bird will take you to the land where he lives," said a pixie. "There you will find an old dame in an old cottage, and she will tell you which way to go next."

"Oh, thank you," said Peter. "Where can I find the Blue Bird?"

"We'll get him for you," said the little folk. One of them took out a silver whistle from his pocket, and blew seven blasts on it. In a few moments there came the sound of flapping wings and a great blue bird soared over the market place. It flew down among the little folk and they ran to it.

"Blue Bird, we want your help," they cried. "Will you take this boy to the Land of Higgledy, where Sly-One the Gnome lives? His sister has been carried off there and he wants to rescue her."

"Certainly," said the bird. "Jump on."

So Peter and Bonzo climbed up on the Blue Bird's soft, feathery back. He spread his broad wings, and flew off into the air. Peter held tight, and Bonzo whined, for he was rather frightened.

"It's a good way off," said the Blue Bird. "It will take quite half an hour to get there. Feel about behind my neck and you'll find a box of chocolate biscuits. You may help yourself."

Peter did as he was told. He soon found the box and opened it. Inside was the finest collection of chocolate biscuits he had ever tasted, and he did wish Betty could have shared them. He gave Bonzo three, and the little dog crunched them all up.

In half an hour's time the Blue Bird turned his head round once more and spoke to Peter.

"We're nearly there," he said. "Can you see some of the houses?"

Peter looked down. He saw a very curious land. All the trees and houses were higgledy-piggledy. The trees grew twisted and crooked, the houses were built in crooked rows, and their windows and chimneys were set higgledy-piggledy anywhere.

The bird flew down to the ground, and Peter and Bonzo got off his back.

"Thank you very much," said Peter. "It was very good of you."

"Don't mention it," said the Blue Bird. "Take one of my feathers, little boy, and put it into your pocket. It may be useful to you, for whenever you want to know where anything is it will at once point in the right direction."

"Oh, thank you," said Peter, and he pulled a little blue feather from the bird's neck. He put

it into his pocket, said good-bye, and then looked about for the old cottage that the little folk had told him about.

It was just a little way off, standing by the side of a lane. It was all crooked, and looked as if it might tumble down at any moment. An old woman stood at the gate, knitting. Peter went up to her.

"Please," he said, "could you tell me the way to the castle of Sly-One the Gnome?"

"I should advise you not to go there," said the old dame, knitting very fast indeed. "He is a bad lot, that gnome."

"I know," said Peter. "But he's got my sister, so I'm afraid I must go to him."

"Dear, dear, is that so?" said the old woman. "Well, little boy, catch the bus at the end of the lane, and ask for Cuckoo Corner. Get off there, and look for a green mushroom behind the hedge. Sit on it and wish yourself underground. As soon as you find yourself in the earth, call for Mr. Mole. He will tell you what to do next."

"Thank you," said Peter. Then, hearing the rumbling sound of a bus, he ran up the lane. At the top he saw a wooden bus drawn by rabbits. He got in, sat down on a seat with Bonzo at his feet, and waited for the conductor to give him a ticket. The conductor was a duck, and he asked Peter where he wanted to go.

"Cuckoo Corner," he said. "How much, please?"

"Bless you, we don't charge anything on this bus," said the duck, giving Peter a ticket as large as a postcard. "I'll tell you when we get to Cuckoo Corner."

But Peter didn't need to be told—for at Cuckoo Corner there was a most tremendous noise of cuckoos cuckooing for all they were worth! Peter hopped out of the bus, and looked for the green mushroom behind the hedge. He soon found it and thought it looked very queer.

"I've never seen a green mushroom before," he said to Bonzo. "Come on, puppy. Jump on my knee, or you may get left behind!"

He sat down on the mushroom and wished himself underground. Bonzo gave a bark of fright as he felt himself sinking downwards, and Peter lost all his breath. Down they went and down. Then bump! They came to rest in a cave far underground. It was lighted by glow-worms who sat in little lamps all about the cave. Peter jumped off the mushroom.

"Now, where's Mister Mole?" he thought. He looked round but could see no one.

"Mister Mole!" he shouted. "Mister Mole! Where are you?"

"Wuff! Mister Mole!" Bonzo shouted too.

Suddenly a door opened in the wall of the cave and a mole with spectacles on his nose looked out.

"Here I am," he said. "What do you want?"

"Please will you help me?" said Peter. "I want to rescue my sister from Sly-One the Gnome and I don't know what to do next."

"Well, this door leads to the cellars of Sly-One's castle," said the mole. "Come with me."

Peter followed the mole through the door, and found himself in a large cellar which seemed never-ending. Boxes and bottles stood all about, and, except for the glow-worms in lamps, the place was quite dark.

The mole led him to some steps.

"If you go up there you'll come to the gnome's kitchen," he said. "Go quietly, because there is someone there. You can hear footsteps on the floor above, if you listen."

Peter listened, and sure enough he heard someone walking about overhead. He felt rather frightened. Suppose it should be the gnome?

He went quietly up the steps—and then, oh dear! Bonzo suddenly gave a whine and darted right up them, ahead of Peter. He disappeared through a door at the top, and Peter was left alone. He looked upwards in dismay.

"How stupid of Bonzo!" he thought. "If that was the gnome, he'll be warned, and will be waiting for me at the top! Well, I can't help it! Here goes!"

Quietly he climbed the rest of the steps, and came to the door, which was half open. He listened, and thought that he heard someone crying. He popped his head suddenly round the door—and, oh my, whoever should he see but Betty herself in a large kitchen, crying and laughing over Bonzo, who was licking her face in excitement.

"Betty!" cried Peter, and he ran to her and hugged her. How glad she was to see him!

"That horrid gnome brought me to his castle and took me to this kitchen," said Betty. "He says I'm to scrub the floor and cook his dinner. Oh, Peter, how can we escape from here?"

"I'll find a way!" said Peter, bravely—but just as he said that his heart sank almost to his boots, for who should come stamping into the kitchen at that very moment but the horrid gnome himself!

"Ha!" he said in surprise, when he saw Peter. "So you think you'll rescue your sister, do you? Well, you're mistaken. There are no doors to this castle, and only one window, which is right at the

very top! You can't get out of there! As for this cellar door which you came here by, I'll lock it this very instant! Now I shall have two servants instead of one! Well, you can start work at once. Scrub the floor, please. Aha! What a lot of work the two of you will be able to do for me!"

Peter watched him in dismay. He locked the cellar door with a large key, pulled Betty's hair, boxed Peter on the ears, and went out of the kitchen, whistling.

Betty began to cry again.

"Don't be frightened," said Peter. "There must be some way out!"

He looked round the kitchen. It had no window, and no door led outside. He ran into the hall. That had no door and no window either. There was another room opposite, and Peter looked into it. It was no use—there wasn't a single door that led outside, and not a window to be seen. The rooms were all lighted by candles that shone brightly in big silver candle-sticks.

The gnome came into the kitchen again, and when he saw that Peter and Betty had done nothing he fell into a rage.

"Now, set to work!" he cried. "If my dinner isn't ready in ten minutes I'll turn you both into beetles. Fry me some bacon and eggs, make me some tea, and toast me some bread!"

He stamped out of the kitchen and left the children in a panic. Neither of them knew how to fry bacon and eggs. But Bonzo came to the rescue.

"I've often watched Cook," he said. "I'll do the bacon and eggs, if you'll make the tea and the toast."

So all three set to work, and soon the gnome's meal was ready on a tray. Peter took the tray in his hands and went into the hall. The gnome looked over the banisters of the staircase, and told him to bring it up to him. Peter carried it up and the gnome led the way to a tiny room whose walls were lined all round with big magic books.

He set the tray on the table and then ran down to Betty again.

"If we're to escape, we'd better do it now!" he said. "The gnome's busy eating."

"But how can we get away?" asked Betty. "There's no way we can go."

"If we only knew where the magic carpet was!" said Peter.

"I say!" suddenly cried Bonzo. "What about that feather the Blue Bird gave you, Peter? Can't you use that to find the carpet?"

"Of course!" cried Peter, and he took the feather from his pocket. He held it up in the air, and spoke to it. "Point to where the magic carpet is!" he commanded. At once the feather twisted round in Peter's hand and pointed towards the door that led into the hall.

"Come on," cried Peter. "It will show us the way!"

They all went into the hall. Then the feather pointed up the stairs. So up they all went, keeping as quiet as they could in case the gnome heard them. Past the door where he was eating his meal they went, and up more stairs. Still the feather pointed upwards. So up they went. At last they came to a broad landing, and on it stood a big chest. The blue feather pointed to it.

Betty ran to the chest and opened it. Inside lay the magic carpet. With a cry of joy she unrolled it and laid it on the floor. And at that very moment the gnome came rushing up the stairs.

"Ho!" he cried. "So that is what you're doing!"

"Quick, quick!" cried Peter, pulling Betty on to the carpet. The gnome rushed up to them — and then brave Bonzo rushed at the gnome, growling fiercely.

"Keep back or I'll bite you!" he said.

The gnome crouched back against the wall, frightened.

"Bonzo, Bonzo, come on to the carpet!" cried Peter. "We must go whilst we can!"

"I can't," said Bonzo. "I must keep the gnome safely in a corner whilst you go. Never mind me."

So Peter spoke the magic word, though he was dreadfully sorry to leave brave Bonzo behind — but he knew that he must rescue Betty whilst he could.

"Arra-gitty-borra-ba!" he cried. "Take us home again!"

At once the carpet rose from the ground and flew upwards. It went up staircase after staircase, for the castle was very tall. At last it came to a big open window right at the very top and flew out. And just then Peter heard Bonzo barking, and caught the sound of his feet tearing up the stairs.

"Wait, wait!" he said to the carpet. "Wait for Bonzo!" But the carpet didn't wait. It flew right out of the window and began to sail away to the east. Peter was in despair.

Bonzo appeared at the window — and, oh my, whatever do you think he did? He saw the carpet sailing away, and he jumped! It was a most tremendous jump, and he nearly missed the carpet! As it was, he wouldn't have got there safely if Peter hadn't caught his tail and pulled him on.

"Oh dear, oh dear!" said Betty, the tears pouring down her cheeks. "I really thought we had lost you, dear Bonzo, darling Bonzo!"

She hugged him and hugged him, and so did Peter.

"You are the bravest puppy I ever knew," said Peter. "Did you bite the gnome?"

"Yes, I did," said Bonzo. "He tried to get past me to go after you, so I bit his ankle. He cried out in rage and ran down the stairs to get a bandage. So I tore up the stairs to try and catch you up."

How happy they all were to be going home together! They passed right over Fairyland, and soon came to their own land. It was not long before they were over their own garden, and the carpet flew down to their nursery window. In a moment they all got off, and danced round in delight.

"Bonzo, can you still talk?" asked Betty.

"Wuff, wuff, wuff!" said Bonzo.

"Oh, you can't!" said Peter. "But never mind, we understand your barks. Now what shall we do with the magic carpet?"

"If we keep it I'm sure that nasty gnome will come after it again," said Betty. "Let's send it away in the air by itself! We shan't want to use it again after all our adventures, I'm sure."

"All right," said Peter. He spoke to the carpet.

"Arra-gitty-borra-ba!" he said. "Rise up in the air and fly round and round the world!"

At once the carpet rose and flew out of the window. It was soon out of sight, and the children sighed with relief.

"That's the end of that!" they said. "What an adventure! Let's go and tell Mummy about it!"

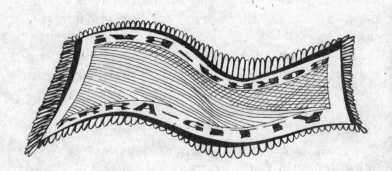

The Little Toy Maker

George and Fanny were excited because Mummy had said they might go out for a picnic by themselves.

"If you cross over the road very carefully and go to the hill above the Long Field, you should be all right," said Mummy.

So they set off, George carrying the basket because he was the boy. In the basket were some egg sandwiches, two rosy apples, a small bar of chocolate, and two pieces of ginger cake. There was a bottle of lemonade as well, and George and Fanny kept thinking of the cool lemonade as they crossed the road, went through the Long Field and up the hill. They did feel so very thirsty!

There were ash and sycamore trees up on the hill. Already they were throwing down their seeds on the wind—ash spinners that spun in the breeze, and sycamore keys that twirled down to the ground. George picked some up and looked at them.

"Aren't they nice?" he said. "Throw some up into the air, Fanny, and see them spin in the wind to the ground. The tree is pleased to see them twirling in the wind, because then it knows that its seeds are travelling far away to grow into big new trees."

After a while the children sat down to have their lunch. They began on the egg sandwiches, but before they had taken more than a few bites they saw a most surprising sight. A very small man, not much higher than George's teddy-bear at home, came walking out from behind a gorse bush. He carried two baskets with him. One was empty and one was full. The full one had sandwiches and milk in it, and the children

36

thought that the small man must be having a picnic, just as they were.

The little man didn't see them. He had a very long white beard that he had tied neatly round his waist to keep out of the way of his feet. He wore enormous glasses on his big nose, and he had funny pointed ears and a hat that had tiny bells on. The bells tinkled as he walked. Fanny wished and wished she had a hat like that.

"What a very little man!" said Fanny. "Do you suppose he is a pixie or a brownie?"

"Sh!" said George. "Don't talk. Let's watch."

So they watched. The little man walked along humming a song—and suddenly he tripped over a root, and down he went! His full basket tipped up, and out fell his sandwiches and milk. The bottle broke. The sandwiches split open and fell into bits on the grass.

"Oh! what a pity!" cried George, and ran to help at once. The little man was surprised to see him. George picked him up, brushed the grass off his clothes, and looked sadly at the milk and sandwiches.

"Your picnic is no use," he said. "Come and share ours. Do!"

The small man smiled and his face lighted up at once. He picked up his baskets and went to where the children had spread their picnic food. Soon he was sitting down chatting to them, sharing their sandwiches, cake, and chocolate. He was very pleased.

"Why was one of your baskets empty?" asked Fanny. "What were you going to put into it?"

"Ash and sycamore keys," said the small man. "There are plenty on this hill."

"Shall we help you to fill your basket?" said George. "We've eaten everything now, and Fanny and I would like to help you."

"Oh, do," said the small man. So the three of them picked up the ash and sycamore keys, and put them neatly into the basket.

"Why do you collect these?" asked Fanny. "I would so like to know. Do you burn them or something?"

"Oh no. I'm a toy-maker and I use them for keys for my clockwork toys," said the little man. "Come along home with me, if you like. I'll show you what I do."

He took them over the top of the hill and there, under a mossy curtain, was a tiny green door set in the side of the hill. The little man pushed a sycamore key into the door and unlocked it. Inside was a tiny room, set with small furniture and a big work-table.

And on the table were all kinds of toys! They were made out of hazel-nut shells, acorns, chestnuts, pine-cones, and all sorts of things! The small man had cleverly made bodies and heads and legs and wings and there were the toys, very small, but very quaint and beautiful. The children stared at them in delight.

"Now, you see," said the little man, emptying

out his basket of keys on to his work-table, "now, you see, all I need to do is to find keys to fit these toys, and then they can be wound up, and they will walk and run and dance. Just fit a few keys into the holes and see if you can wind up any of the toys."

In great excitement the two children fitted ash and sycamore keys into the toys, and George found one that fitted a pine-cone bird perfectly. He wound it up—and the bird danced and hopped, pecked and even flapped its funny wings. It was lovely to watch.

Soon all the quaint toys were dancing about on the table, and the children clapped their hands in joy. It was the funniest sight they had ever seen! They only had to fit a key to any of the toys, wind it up—and lo and behold, that toy came to life!

"I wish we hadn't got to go, but we must," said George at last. "Goodbye, little fellow. I do love your toys."

"Choose one each!" said the little man generously. So they did. Fanny chose the bird, and George chose a hedgehog made very cleverly out of a prickly chestnut-case and a piece of beech-mast. It ran just as a real hedgehog does when George wound it up.

And now those two quaint toys are on their nursery mantelpiece at home, and they are so funny to watch when George and Fanny wind them up with ash and sycamore keys. I can't show you the toys—but you can go and find ash and sycamore keys in the autumn for yourself if you like. There are plenty under the trees, spinning in the wind. Find a few, and see what good little keys they make for winding up fairy toys!

Angelina and the Toy Balloon

Wilfrid and Mollie were playing in the garden with a new air-balloon. It was very big. The wind tossed it here and there, and if it had not been tied tightly to a string held by Wilfrid, it would have been blown away. Just then Nurse called the children in.

"Auntie Nora has come and wants to see you," she said. "Leave your toys out there, and come in for a moment. You can go back to them afterwards."

The two children looked about for somewhere safe to leave the balloon. They were afraid that the wind might blow it away.

"I know," said Mollie. "Let's tie it round my doll's waist. Angelina shall hold it safely for us till we come back."

So they tied the balloon string tightly round Angelina's waist, and then ran indoors to see their Auntie Nora.

But when they had gone the wind began to blow a regular gale! It blew and it blew, and the balloon tossed about in the air, and tried its hardest to get away. But the string was strong and would not break.

Then the wind blew harder still and, oh dear me, whatever do you think happened? Why, the balloon was blown high into the air, and pulled poor Angelina the doll with it! There she flew swiftly, dragged after the balloon, very frightened indeed.

When she looked down she could see the houses and gardens, and they looked very small, just like dolls' houses and toy farms. Angelina wondered if she would fly as high as the moon, and she hoped that the string would not break, for she knew that if it did she would tumble to the ground with a nasty bump.

The balloon flew on and on in the wind. It sailed over fields and hills and soon it came to where a big town began. Then it sailed over chimneys and more chimneys and still more chimneys. Angelina was nearly choked with the smoke that came out of them.

The wind dropped, and the balloon began to drift downwards. A bird flying by bumped into it, and was very much surprised. He flew off in a hurry, wondering whatever it was that he had flown into.

His beak had made a tiny hole in the big red balloon. The air escaped through it very slowly and made a little hissing sound over Angelina's head.

"Oh my, oh my, the balloon is going flat, and I shall soon fall!" she thought in a fright. "Whatever shall I do? Oh, Mollie! Oh, Wilfrid! I shall never see you again, you dear, kind children! I am quite lost!"

Two tears ran down her little china nose. The balloon got smaller and smaller, and dropped down very low indeed. Then it gave one last sigh and fell down to a chimney. Angelina fell, too — but she slipped right into the chimney itself, and the string broke. Down she went, and down and down. It was very dark and Angelina was frightened.

Suddenly she came to rest with a thud. She was lying on some crumpled newspaper in a fireplace. There was no fire there, but only just the paper and a few sticks laid ready for when it was next to be lighted. Angelina wasn't hurt a bit.

There was a man in the room and he looked in surprise when he heard the thud. When he saw Angelina sitting in the fireplace, all sooty and black, he was very much astonished.

"Well!" he said. "I never in my life heard of a doll tumbling down the chimney! I must take you home to my children and tell them how you came to me!"

He picked Angelina up and sat her in a chair. When the time came for him to go home again, he popped the doll into his bag. In an hour's

44

time he was walking up his front garden path, with poor Angelina wondering what kind of strange children she would have to meet.

"Here's Daddy, here's Daddy!" cried gay voices, and two children dragged their father into the house.

"I've brought you something," said the man. "It's a doll that fell down my chimney in the office today. Isn't that a strange thing!"

He opened his case and took Angelina out. He gave her to a little girl—and oh, whatever do you think! The little girl was Mollie herself—and by her was Wilfrid, looking at Angelina in the greatest astonishment.

45

"Why, it's our own dear Angelina!" cried Mollie in delight. "Oh, Daddy! What a funny thing! Our balloon took her away today, and we saw her disappearing through the air. The wind must have taken her to your office in town and dropped her down your chimney! Would you believe it?"

Wasn't Angelina glad to find that she was home again after all her adventures! Mollie carried her off to have a bath, and soon she was in her own little bed and fast asleep.

"Poor little doll!" said Mollie, covering her up with a pink blanket. "What a terrible fright she must have had. Well, we won't tie her to a balloon again, will we, Wilfrid?"

Betsy-May and the Bear

Betsy-May had a beautiful doll's pram. It was green and had a hood that went up and down like the hood on her baby-brother's pram. It had a brake too, and a shining handle. It was really lovely.

Betsy-May took her dolls and her bear out every single day in the pram. She said they liked an outing as much as Baby James.

"Teddy-bear likes it best of all," she told her mother. "He needs fresh air. He told me so."

"Did he really?" said her mother. "Well, he is a most sensible bear then. He knows what is best for bears and little girls too. You must take him out every day, Betsy-May."

Now one day something went wrong with Betsy-May's doll's pram. A big screw fell out and Betsy-May didn't notice it. Then a wheel came loose because the screw wasn't there, and at last it came right off. Betsy-May was most upset.

"Now don't get worried," said Mummy. "We will take it to the bicycle-shop and leave it there

to be mended. It will only take a little while."

But the bicycle-man was very busy mending bicycles, and he said it would be two days before the pram was mended. Betsy-May was sorry.

"My dolls and my bear will miss going out for their walk," she told the man. "Can't you mend it to-day, please?"

"No, I can't, Missy," said the man. "Your dolls and your bear had better have a cold and stay in bed to-day and to-morrow. Then they won't mind not going out."

"They've only just *had* colds," said Betsy-May. "They can't have another one just yet. Well, never mind. They must be patient."

Betsy-May went to look at her dolls and her bear the next day. "I am very, very sorry not to be able to take you out," she said. "But the pram isn't mended yet. I do hope you won't mind very much."

The dolls looked up at her with smiling faces. But the bear didn't smile. Betsy-May looked at him. She thought he really looked very sad.

"Cheer up," she said. "It's only to-day and to-morrow you can't go out."

But the bear still looked very sad. Betsy-May quite expected to see tears running out of his eyes, but he was brave enough not to cry.

Betsy-May felt unhappy because her bear was unhappy. He came to bed with her every night, and he was her favourite toy. He was so soft and cuddlesome, and he had such a nice friendly face. She went to nurse and told her.

"He looks dreadfully sad," she said. "I do wish I could borrow a pram from somewhere. I suppose you wouldn't let me have Baby's pram, would you? I'd be very careful."

"Good gracious, no!" said nurse. "If you so badly want to take your bear out, why don't you put a cushion into your little barrow, and a rug or two, and take the bear out in that?"

"That *is* a good idea!" said Betsy-May in delight. "I'll get it."

So she got the little barrow and made a nice bed inside it with a little pillow, a tiny mattress, a sheet, and a rug.

"What shall I do for a hood?" she wondered. "He must have a hood over him, because of the sun. He doesn't like the sun in his eyes. Oh — I know! I'll get a little umbrella — my own one — and put it up for the hood."

So she did. Really, the barrow looked fine, almost like a pram!

Betsy-May set off with the barrow-pram. She went down the garden, and out of the gate at the bottom into the quiet little lane. She wheeled the barrow along for a good way and then she met Mrs. Jordans.

"Good morning, Betsy-May," said Mrs. Jordans. "That's a funny pram you have this morning! Which doll are you taking for a walk?"

"It's my teddy-bear," said Betsy-May. "He's under the umbrella. That's for a hood, you see."

Mrs. Jordans peeped under the umbrella. Then she lifted it a little and peeped again.

"Well, that's funny," she said, "I can't see him!"

Betsy-May lifted up the umbrella in alarm. Goodness gracious, there was no bear there! How very astonishing!

"Where's he gone?" cried Betsy-May. "Oh, Mrs. Jordans, please help me to look for him! He's my own darling favourite bear, and he goes to bed with me at night. Oh, where can he be? Do you think he jumped out of the barrow because he didn't like it?"

"I shouldn't really think so," said Mrs. Jordans.

Betsy-May looked up and down the lane, hoping to see a small bear running away. But there wasn't one to be seen. She began to cry bitterly.

"Oh, he's gone! I've lost him! I only took him out in the barrow because he looked so sad. And

now he's quite, quite lost."

Mrs. Jordans tried to comfort Betsy-May, but the little girl pushed away her hand and ran home. She ran up the garden, sobbing loudly. Nurse looked out of the nursery window, most alarmed.

"Betsy-May, have you hurt yourself?" she called. "What's the matter?"

Betsy-May rushed upstairs to nurse, still crying. "Oh, a dreadful thing has happened!" she wept. "I've lost Teddy. He's gone. He jumped out of my barrow."

Nurse looked at Betsy-May and laughed. "Then he must have run back home very quickly," she said. "Because there he is on that chair."

Betsy-May looked at the chair—and sure enough, there was the teddy-bear sitting on the

51

chair, with a little straw hat on his head, and a little scarf round his neck.

"Oh! The darling! He's here after all!" squealed Betsy-May, and she ran to the bear and took him up to hug him. "Oh, did you run all the way back? Oh, how glad I am to have you again!"

Betsy-May sat down on the chair with the bear and thought hard. She went very red.

"What's the matter now?" asked nurse.

"Do you know, I'm a very silly girl," said Betsy-May in a rather small voice. "I don't believe I put Teddy into the barrow at all. I arranged it all so beautifully for him and put the umbrella on top for a hood—and then I went off without him! I couldn't see he wasn't there, because of the umbrella. Do you think he thinks I'm very silly?"

"No, I should think he feels as I do—that you really are the funniest child in the world!" said nurse. "I should think he wants to laugh, just as I do!"

And when Betsy-May looked at the bear, he didn't look sad any more. He really did look as if he wanted to laugh! And I'm not surprised at that, are you?

The Good Old Rocking Horse

In the nursery there was a big old rocking-horse. His name was Dobbin, and he was on rockers that went to and fro, to and fro, when anyone rode on him.

He was a dear old horse, and it was very queer that the toys didn't like him! They were afraid of him—and it was all because of something that was quite an accident.

It happened like this. One day the toy monkey fell off the shelf nearby, and went bump on to the floor. His long tail spread itself out, and a bit of it went under one of the rocking-horse's rockers.

Well, that didn't matter a bit—until John got up on to the horse and rocked to and fro. Then, of course, the rocking-horse pinched the monkey's tail hard every time he rocked over it, and the monkey sobbed and cried after John had gone to bed.

"You great big, unkind thing!" sobbed the poor monkey, holding his tail between his paws. "You nearly squashed my tail in half. You hurt me dreadfully. I nearly squealed out loud when John was riding you. I don't like you one bit."

"Listen, monkey," said the rocking-horse in his deep, gentle voice, "I didn't mean to do that. I didn't even know that your tail was there. And in any case I couldn't help it, because John rocked me so hard. But do believe me when I say that I am very, very sorry. I wouldn't have hurt you for the world!"

"I should just think you *are* sorry!" wept the monkey. "Oh my poor tail! Whatever shall I do with it?"

The golliwog came up with a bandage. The baby-doll came up with a bowl of water. They bathed the tail and then bound up the squashed end with the bandage. The monkey looked at his tail and felt rather grand when he saw how important it looked with a bandage round it.

It was quite better after a time—but somehow the toys really never forgave the rocking-horse, and he was very sad about it. He knew that he couldn't have helped rocking over the monkey's tail—it was really John's fault for leaving his monkey on the floor—but the toys never seemed to understand that.

So they didn't ask Dobbin to play games with them, and they never even said "yes," when he asked them to have a ride on his back. They just shook their heads and said "no." This hurt the rocking-horse very much, because there was nothing he liked better than giving people rides.

"They think I'm unkind, though I'm not," he thought sadly. "Well—I suppose they will always think the same and I must just put up with it."

Now the toys were very friendly with a little red squirrel who lived in the pine-trees at the bottom of the garden. He often used to come leaping up to the window-sill to talk to them. Sometimes he even came right into the nursery, and he was delighted one day when they got out one of the dolls' hair-brushes and brushed his beautiful bushy tail for him.

"Oh, thank you," he said. "Thank you very

much indeed. That's so kind of you. I'll bring you a present one day, Toys."

So when the autumn came he brought them a present. It was two pawfuls of nuts! He had picked them from the hazel trees for the toys.

"Here you are," he said. "Nuts for you. They are most delicious! You must crack the hard shell and inside you will find a lovely white nut. I do hope you will like them. Good-bye!"

He sprang off to find some nuts for himself. He meant to hide some in cracks and corners, so that if he awoke in the cold winter days he might find his nuts and have a meal.

The toys looked at the nuts. They were so excited and pleased because they didn't often get any presents. They longed to eat the nuts and see what they tasted like.

The golly put one into his mouth and tried to crack the shell. But he couldn't. It was much too hard. Then the brown toy dog tried to crack one. But even he couldn't! Then the toys threw the nuts hard on to the floor, but not one cracked.

"We shan't be able to eat the nuts," said the brown dog sadly. "They will be wasted!"

"Let us get the little hammer out of the toy tool-box," said the bear. "Perhaps we can break the nuts with that."

So they looked for the toy hammer and they found it. They put a nut on the floor and hit hard with the hammer. But the nut jumped away each time, unbroken. It was most tiresome.

Then the rocking-horse spoke up in his deep, gentle voice. "I can crack your nuts for you, Toys! If you will put them underneath my rockers I can rock over them and crack the shells! One of you must ride me to and fro, and then I can easily crack the nuts for you."

The toys all looked at one another. They badly

wanted their nuts cracked, so they thought they would do as Dobbin said. They laid all the nuts in a row under his rockers. Then the golliwog climbed up on the horse's back and began to rock him to and fro.

Crick-crack, crick-crack went all the nuts as the shells broke. Inside were the lovely white kernels, so sweet and delicious to eat!

"Thank you, Dobbin!" said the toys. The golliwog patted him and slid down to get his nuts.

"That was a lovely ride I had!" he whispered to the other toys. "I wouldn't mind another!"

"Have as many as you like!" said Dobbin, who heard what the golly said. "Are the nuts nice?"

"Delicious! Have one?" said the bear, and he held one up for Dobbin to nibble. "It was kind of you to crack them for us — very friendly indeed."

"I'm such a friendly person," said the rocking-horse sadly, "but you won't make friends with me. I would so much like to give you all a ride."

He looked so sad that the monkey suddenly felt very sorry for him. In a trice he had leapt up on to Dobbin's back.

"Gee-up!" he cried. "I'll be friends with you! Gee-up!"

And then, one after another, all the toys had a ride, and after that they were as friendly as could be. Wasn't it a good thing Dobbin offered to crack their nuts for them?

The New Doll

Who do you suppose is in
My dolly's cot to-day?
Come and pull the cover back
Just a little way.

Yes, it's Pussy lying there,
A night-cap on her head,
I put her in and tucked her up,
She loves her cosy bed!

But Dolly's rather cross — she sulks —
And when I've gone to play
I'm sure she'll turn my pussy out
And send her right away!